RAINBOW magic ®

The Green Fairies

Special thanks to
Narinder Dhami

ORCHARD BOOKS
338 Euston Road, London NW1 3BH
Orchard Books Australia
Level 17/207 Kent Street, Sydney, NSW 2000

A Paperback Original
First published in 2009 by Orchard Books.

A CIP catalogue record for this book is available
from the British Library.

ISBN 978 1 40830 479 2
1 3 5 7 9 10 8 6 4 2

Printed and bound in China by Imago

The paper and board used in this paperback are natural recyclable
products made from wood grown in sustainable forests. The
manufacturing processes conform to the environmental regulations
of the country of origin.

Orchard Books is a division of Hachette Children's Books,
an Hachette UK company

www.hachette.co.uk

Carrie
the Snow Cap
Fairy

by Daisy Meadows

ORCHARD

www.rainbowmagic.co.uk

Jack Frost's Ice Castle

Rainspell Island

Wildlife Garden

Lake

Holiday Cottage

Beach

Harbour

The Coral Reef

Ice Cap

The fairies must be in a dream
If they think they can be called 'green'.
My goblin servants are definitely greenest
And I, of course, am by far the meanest.

Seven fairies out to save the Earth?
This idea fills me full of mirth.
I'm sure the world has had enough
Of fairy magic and all that stuff.

So I'm going to steal the fairies' wands
And send them into human lands.
The fairies will think all is lost

Defeated again, by me, Jack Frost!

Contents

Frosty Leaves

"Brr!" Shivering, Rachel Walker glanced across the bedroom at her best friend, Kirsty Tate, who was just waking up too. "It's really cold this morning, isn't it?"

Kirsty yawned and nodded. "It's freezing," she agreed. "It's been getting colder all week."

9

"Well, I suppose it *is* the end of
October," said Rachel.
She sat up in
bed, wrapping
the duvet around
her shoulders.
"It'll be
winter soon
– but I didn't
expect the weather
to change quite so fast!"

"Haven't we had a lovely holiday
though, Rachel?" Kirsty sighed happily.
"It's been so special to come back to
Rainspell Island, where we first met."

The Walkers and the Tates were
spending the autumn half-term holiday
together in a pretty little cottage on
beautiful, magical Rainspell Island.

"Yes, it's been brilliant!" Rachel smiled.
"And we're even
having another fairy
adventure, just like
we did the first
time we visited
Rainspell."

"Only this
time it was
our turn to ask
the fairies for
help," Kirsty pointed out.

When Kirsty and Rachel had returned
to Rainspell Island a week ago, they'd
been horrified to see the wide, golden
beach covered in litter. So they'd asked
the king and queen of Fairyland if their
fairy friends could help them to clean
up the human environment.

The king and queen had explained to
the girls that fairy magic could only do
so much, and that humans had to help
the environment, too. But they had agreed
that the seven fairies who were about to
complete their training could become the
Green Fairies for a trial period. The Green
Fairies would work together with Rachel
and Kirsty to try to make the world a
cleaner place. If the fairies completed
their training successfully, they would
become permanent.

But just as the Green Fairies were about
to be presented with their new wands, Jack
Frost and his goblins had zoomed towards
them on a ice bolt. The goblins had
snatched all seven wands, and then Jack
Frost's icy magic had sent them tumbling
away into the human world.

Jack Frost had declared that the world didn't need any more do-gooder fairies, but Rachel and Kirsty had promised they would do their best to get all the wands back into the safe hands of the Green Fairies.

"Wasn't it *just* like Jack Frost and his naughty goblin servants to steal all the wands?" Kirsty said, shuddering at the memory. "Thank goodness we've managed to find six of them, Rachel."

"Yes, with the help of Nicole, Isabella, Edie, Coral, Lily and Milly," Rachel replied. "But we still have to find Carrie the Snow Cap Fairy's wand."

Kirsty looked worried. "If we don't find Carrie's wand, the fairies will fail their final exam, and even worse, they won't be able to carry on helping the environment."

"But you know what Queen Titania always says," Rachel reminded Kirsty as she went over to draw the curtains, "we have to wait for the magic to come to *us*."

"I know," Kirsty said with a sigh. "But we don't have much time – we're going home later today."

As Rachel opened the curtains wide, she gave a surprised gasp.

"Kirsty, come and look!"

Kirsty ran to join Rachel at the window. There had been a heavy frost during the night, and the trees, flowers and grass in the cottage garden were covered with a thin layer of white ice that glittered  in the morning sunshine.

"Doesn't the garden look beautiful?" Kirsty exclaimed.

"Let's go out before it all melts," Rachel suggested.

The girls dressed quickly and ran downstairs. The front door of the cottage was open and Mr Walker was sprinkling salt on the path to melt the ice.

"Morning, girls," he said as Rachel and Kirsty stepped outside. "Be careful you don't slip."

"We won't," Rachel replied. But as she spoke, her foot slid away from her, and Kirsty had to grab her arm to stop her falling over.

Rachel's dad grinned. "See what I mean?"

"Why do you think it's got so cold all of a sudden, Mr Walker?" asked Kirsty.

"I suppose it's because of global warming," Mr Walker replied, scattering a handful of salt across the path.

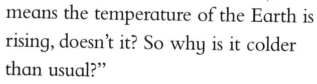

"Global warming," Kirsty repeated thoughtfully. "That means the temperature of the Earth is rising, doesn't it? So why is it colder than usual?"

"Global warming can cause some strange weather – too cold, too hot, too wet. Overall though, the world is getting hotter. Even the polar ice caps are melting," Mr Walker explained. "That's very bad news for the world because it means in years to come the seas will rise, and then there might be floods." He emptied out the last grains of salt, then glanced at his watch. "I must go and help with the packing. We're leaving soon."

Rachel turned to Kirsty as Mr Walker hurried into the house.

"We *must* find Carrie's wand before we leave Rainspell Island," Rachel whispered.

"We need her help to fight global warming!"

"We'll just have to keep our eyes open," replied Kirsty, glancing around. "The garden looks so pretty, doesn't it, Rachel? The frost is making everything sparkle in the sunshine."

"Look at the frosty leaves on that plant." Rachel pointed further down the garden. "They almost seem to be glowing!"

The girls went to take a closer look. As they got nearer, they could see something fluttering around the leaves. At first, they thought it was a butterfly. But then Kirsty grabbed Rachel's arm, her face full of excitement.

"I can see a fairy!" Kirsty cried.

The fairy was dressed in
a green fake-fur jacket over the top of a
cosy wool jumper. She wore mittens, and
dark blue jeans tucked into furry boots.
She was hovering above a frosty leaf, and
as Rachel and Kirsty watched, the fairy
gently kissed its surface. Instantly the frost
melted away, and the leaf glowed green.

Suddenly the fairy spotted Rachel and
Kirsty and waved.

"Girls!" she called. "Do you remember
me? I'm Carrie the Snow Cap Fairy!"

Goblins on Ice

"Of course we remember you, Carrie!"
Rachel said.

"We're so pleased to see you," Kirsty
added with a smile.

"And I'm pleased to see *you*," declared
Carrie, zooming over to them. "Girls,
I desperately need my wand back! The
polar ice caps are melting, and I *have*
to try to stop that happening."

"Have you any idea where your wand is?" asked Rachel.

Carrie nodded. "Oh, yes," she replied.

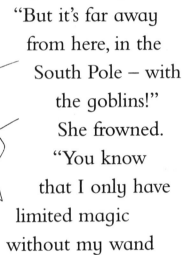

"But it's far away from here, in the South Pole – with the goblins!" She frowned. "You know that I only have limited magic without my wand because I'm still a fairy-in-training. So I'll have to use what little magic I have to get us there."

"We're coming with you!" Kirsty said in a determined voice, and Rachel nodded.

Carrie sighed with relief. "Then let's go, girls!" she cried. "There's no time to lose."

Carrie fluttered above Rachel and Kirsty, waving her hands and whispering some magic words. A shower of magical fairy dust floated down around the girls, and as it did so the frosty garden began to shimmer and sparkle even more brightly in the sunshine. Rachel and Kirsty were dazzled and had to close their eyes. The next moment they felt themselves being whisked off their feet, and then they were flying through the air.

"We've arrived, girls!" Carrie cried joyfully. "And I've made sure you're going to be warm and cosy, here in my cold but beautiful South Pole!"

Eagerly the girls opened their eyes. Carrie had turned them into fairies with her magic, and they were hovering high up in the air. They were now wearing fluffy white earmuffs, mittens, furry boots and shimmering silver parkas, with glittering fairy wings on their shoulders.

Freezing cold air swirled around
Rachel and Kirsty as they looked down
at the landscape below them. The
girls were utterly amazed
by what they saw.

They were floating
above vast, icy
plains that
stretched in
every direction,
as far as the eye
could see. The
plains were
bordered by an
enormous ocean. The
greenish-blue water was
covered with huge, towering
icebergs and thick flat sheets of
ice that moved slowly across the surface.

In the distance the girls could see snow-covered mountains, their peaks glistening in the pale light of the sun.

"This is so beautiful!" Kirsty gasped. "But there are hardly any plants or trees!"

"That's because the ice never really melts very much, even in summer," Carrie explained. "At certain times of the year, the whole sea freezes over!"

Suddenly, a seal popped his sleek head out of the icy water. He stared curiously up at Carrie and the girls with bright dark eyes.

Then with one swift flick of his tail, he
disappeared again.

"Will we see any polar bears?" Rachel
asked, looking around eagerly.

Carrie laughed. "Animals like polar
bears and walruses, and caribou live in
the *North* Pole!" she told the girls. "But
there are lots of different animals here.
I'll show you around
while we search
for my wand.
Come on!"

Rachel
and Kirsty
quickly
flew after
Carrie as
she whizzed
across the water.

"Look at the icebergs below us," Kirsty said to Rachel. "They're the most amazing shapes!"

"And so big," Rachel added. "They look taller than our cottage back on Rainspell!"

Just then a spray of sea water shot up into the air. Carrie and the girls had to dodge to avoid getting splashed.

"See the blue whale, girls?" Carrie yelled. "That water came from his blowhole!"

Rachel and Kirsty glanced down and just caught a glimpse of the enormous whale as he dived underwater again.

"There's so much to see!" Kirsty exclaimed. It was then she spotted something glinting brightly in the sunshine just ahead of them.

"Oh! What's *that?* " Kirsty cried, pointing it out to Rachel and Carrie.

But when the three friends flew closer, they saw that it was just a long thin icicle hanging from an iceberg.

Kirsty's face fell. "I thought it was the wand," she sighed.

"Listen!" Rachel said suddenly. "I can hear something!"

She spun round in the air, and spotted a large group of penguins standing on an ice sheet not far behind them. The penguins were squawking loudly and seemed very annoyed.

"Let's go and check it out," Carrie suggested.

They flew towards the penguins, but as they got closer, Kirsty gave a cry. "Goblins!" she gasped.

Three goblins were standing on the sheet of ice, surrounded by penguins. They were all arguing loudly.

"I wonder what they're fighting about?" Carrie asked, puzzled. But Kirsty had already spotted something.

"See the big penguin at the front?" Kirsty pointed out, breathless with excitement. "He has your wand, Carrie!"

The penguin was holding the gleaming wand firmly between his black flippers. As one of the goblins lunged to grab it, the other penguins immediately rushed forward, flapping their flippers at the goblin. He retreated hastily, scowling.

"The penguins don't want to give up the wand!" Rachel said with a grin.

The three goblins were muttering
amongst themselves. Suddenly, they all
dashed towards the big
penguin. They
took him by
surprise, and
one of the
goblins managed
to grab the end of
the wand. But the big
penguin, squawking with rage, held
tightly onto the other end.

"They're having a tug of war!" laughed
Kirsty, as the other penguins and goblins
rushed to join the battle for the wand.

The goblins were outnumbered by the
penguins, but they were determined not
to give in. They jumped up and down,
tugging hard at the wand.

Suddenly there was a loud *CRACK!*

"What's that?" Carrie gasped.

"The sheet of ice has cracked in two!" Kirsty shouted.

The ice that the goblins and penguins were standing on had broken away from the main sheet and was floating away. The goblins were thrown off-balance, but the smallest one just managed to wrestle the wand from the big penguin as the three of them fell over.

"I've got it!" the goblin roared triumphantly, waving the wand in the air.

"Give it to *me*!" the others yelled, both trying to grab it.

Looking disgusted with the goblins, the penguins dived into the water and swam off. Meanwhile, the piece of ice continued to float away as the goblins argued over the wand.

"The goblins don't realise it, but they're stranded and floating out to sea!" Rachel exclaimed.

"Yes, they're in great danger," Carrie added anxiously. "And they're taking my wand with them!"

Jack Frost Appears

Carrie, Rachel and Kirsty immediately flew over to the goblins.

"You're in big trouble!" Carrie called down to them. "You're floating right out to sea, and what will you do then?"

The goblins stopped arguing. They looked around them and realised that Carrie was right. Panic spread across their faces.

"HELP!" they shouted loudly.

"Give us the wand, and we'll make sure you get safely back to the shore," Kirsty offered.

The goblins stared suspiciously up at the three friends. Then they went into a little huddle and began muttering to each other.

"We don't need the help of any silly fairies!" the biggest goblin sneered. "Jack Frost is coming very soon to collect the wand."

"Yes, he loves all this ice and snow," the smallest goblin chimed in, waving the wand around. "And he can't *wait* to have another wand for winter."

"Jack Frost must be on his way by now," said the third goblin. "*He'll* help us! So there!" And he poked his tongue out rudely at Carrie and the girls.

"We *must* get the wand back before Jack Frost arrives," Carrie whispered urgently to Rachel and Kirsty.

"Let's fly down and try to snatch it," Rachel suggested.

But as the three friends flew lower, the smallest goblin pointed the wand at them threateningly. "Keep away!" he shouted.

"Or I'll use my magic to stop you!"

"Don't do that!" Carrie warned him.
"The magic is very unpredictable in the
wrong hands—"

But the goblins weren't listening.
The biggest goblin lunged
forward and grabbed the
wand from the other one.
Then he began waving
it wildly in the air,
chanting a silly spell:
"We love ice,
We love snow,
Do we love fairies?
No, no, NO!
We want snowballs,
Not to play,
So we can shoo
These fairies away!"

Carrie and the girls watched anxiously as a few sparkles of fairy dust drifted from the wand. Suddenly an enormous snowball fell from the sky and landed with a *SPLAT* right on top of the goblins. They disappeared from view into the giant pile of snow, and all Carrie and the girls could see were their legs sticking out. The three friends couldn't help laughing as the silly goblins wriggled out of the snow and shook themselves off.

"Get them!" the smallest goblin yelled. Quickly, he rolled some snow into a snowball and hurled it straight at Rachel. She ducked, but now the other two goblins were making snowballs too, and throwing them at Carrie and Kirsty.

"We can't get close enough to grab the wand while they're attacking us!" Kirsty panted, zooming upwards to avoid another snowball.

"Look!" Carrie pointed down at the ocean. "The seals think this is a game!"

The girls glanced down and saw several seals bobbing around in the water. As the snowballs flew, the seals batted them with their flippers, honking with delight whenever they hit one.

Suddenly Rachel noticed a tall thin white figure standing on the icy shore.

"Oh no!" she whispered to Carrie and Kirsty. "It's Jack Frost!"

The goblins hadn't noticed that Jack
Frost had arrived. The biggest one flung
a snowball at Carrie, but he slipped
slightly as he threw it and instead the
snowball whizzed towards the shore. It
hit Jack Frost smack in the face. Carrie,
Rachel and Kirsty grinned at each other.

"STOP!" Jack Frost
roared furiously, wiping
the snow away.

"Oh, no!" the
biggest goblin
muttered,
looking
horrified.

"We knew you'd
come to rescue us,"
the smallest goblin
called to Jack Frost.

Jack Frost scowled. "I've a good mind to let you float right out to sea!" he snapped.

"Sorry! Sorry!" gabbled the biggest goblin. "But look, we have the wand – you should be proud of us!" And he waved it in the air.

"How are we going to get the wand back *now*?" Kirsty whispered in dismay as Jack Frost smiled smugly.

Bridge of Ice

"We'll have to try and persuade him to give my wand back!" Carrie said in a determined voice.

She flew closer to Jack Frost, with Rachel and Kirsty right behind her.

"Actually, that wand belongs to Carrie," Kirsty called to Jack Frost.

"And one way or another we have to get it back," Rachel added bravely. "It's really important for the environment."

Jack Frost burst out laughing. "More silly do-gooder fairies!" he jeered. Then he raised his wand and sent a glittering stream of frosty sparkles shooting towards the sea. As the sparkles whizzed through the air, they formed a bridge from the shore to the ice sheet where the goblins stood.

The goblins whooped and cheered. "Let's go!" the biggest goblin yelled triumphantly, tucking the wand under his arm.

"*I* should give the wand to Jack Frost," the smallest goblin said, scowling at him, "because *I* was the one who got it back from the penguins."

"No way!" the biggest goblin declared.

"Well, I haven't even had a turn at holding the wand yet!" the third goblin complained, trying to grab it from the biggest goblin.

The goblins began fighting over the wand, but suddenly the smallest goblin slipped on the ice.

"Help!" he shouted as he toppled head-first into the freezing ocean.

Meanwhile, the third goblin had managed to grab the wand, and now he rushed across the ice bridge towards Jack Frost. He ignored the goblin in the water, and so did the biggest goblin who dashed after him, shrieking with rage.

"We'd better help him, girls," Carrie said quickly.

The three friends flew down to the goblin who was splashing and spluttering in the cold water.

A group of seals had surrounded him, stopping him from floating further out to sea. Summoning up all of her magic, Carrie managed to push the goblin out of the water and back onto the icy shore. He stood, dripping and shivering, next to Jack Frost and the other goblins.

"I'm grateful to you for helping my goblin servant," Jack Frost called out. "But I still won't give you the wand!"

"Be careful, girls!" Carrie gasped as Jack Frost raised his own wand. "He's going to shoot an ice bolt at us!"

There was a flash of icy white as the ice bolt flew from Jack Frost's wand.

But, to everyone's amazement, it just fell to the ground, landing at Jack Frost's feet with a thud, instead of zipping through the air like the ice bolts usually did.

Frowning, Jack Frost tried again. This time the ice bolt melted and turned to slushy water in midair.

"Look!" the biggest goblin yelled. "The ice bridge is melting, too!"

Jack Frost glared up at Carrie, Rachel and Kirsty hovering a short distance away. "What kind of magic are you using against my icy powers?" he raged.

"We're not using any magic," Carrie replied. "It's global warming!"

"The temperature of the Earth is rising," explained Rachel.

"So the warmer air must be affecting your icy powers," Kirsty pointed out.

"Does this mean I might lose my ice magic?" Jack Frost asked in horror.

Rachel nodded. "If Carrie doesn't get her wand back, there'll be no Green Fairies, and that will be terrible for the environment," she said. "Then you'll just be plain old Jack, instead of Jack Frost!"

Jack Frost was silent for a moment.

"Very well," he muttered at last. "I'll give you your wand back." And he held it out to Carrie.

Looking relieved, Carrie swooped down to take the wand. But at the last moment Jack Frost changed his mind and snatched it away. Carrie tried again, but once more Jack Frost held onto the wand tightly.

"I promise to do my very best to keep the snow and ice caps cold, if you'll give me my wand back," Carrie said earnestly.

"But you and your goblins have to help, too. For instance, you shouldn't be wasting energy, because burning fuel like coal and gas and oil all add to global warming."

"Maybe you could turn off the lights in your Ice Castle," Kirsty suggested.

"And you need to recycle," added Rachel. "Maybe you could transform your magic powers into some kind of icy energy that you could use for fuel in the castle?"

Jack Frost frowned thoughtfully. Carrie, Kirsty and Rachel held their breath.

Had they managed to persuade Jack Frost to hand over the wand and help the environment…?

Go, Green Fairies!

"Well," Jack Frost said with a sigh, "I'll try to think of something. But only because I love the cold, and I can't bear to see my Ice Castle melt. It's nothing to do with helping you pesky fairies!"

Then he handed the wand reluctantly to Carrie.

The moment Carrie touched her wand, a sparkling icy breeze sprang up around the three friends and whisked them off to Fairyland in the blink of an eye.

A few seconds later they landed in the palace gardens. Rachel and Kirsty smiled when they saw the king and queen and Bertram the frog footman waiting for them.

"Welcome back, Carrie, Rachel and Kirsty!" the queen called.

"All the Green Fairies have now passed their final exam," the king announced. "Well done! May I have your wand, please, Carrie?"

Rachel and Kirsty beamed as Carrie handed her wand to the king. He in turn gave the wand to Bertram, who hopped away with it.

"We'll return all the wands when they're full of Fairyland magic," the king explained with a smile. "Now, let's join the other Green Fairies at the Seeing Pool."

They all made their way through the beautiful, colourful palace gardens towards the golden Seeing Pool. Nicole, Isabella, Edie, Coral, Lily and Milly waved excitedly at Rachel, Kirsty and Carrie as they joined them. They all chattered excitedly about their amazing adventures.

After a while, the queen addressed them: "You've made everyone in Fairyland very proud," she declared.

"And now here comes Bertram. Your wands have been powered up, and it's time for the Fairyland Wand Ceremony!"

Bertram hopped forward, carrying a tray of seven wands. Rachel and Kirsty could see that the wands were now glowing with the brightness of the full moon.

As the queen handed Nicole the Beach Fairy her new wand, a rainbow of sparkles burst from the tip of it. Rachel and Kirsty gasped with delight as the sparkles zoomed up into the sky and floated there on the breeze. This happened six more times as the other six fairies were presented with their wands. Then all the sparkles formed themselves into a glittering, luminous rainbow, high in the sky above Fairyland.

"Congratulations!" the queen told the Green Fairies, as Rachel and Kirsty applauded. "You've all done very well, but there's more work to do."

Smiling, the seven fairies fluttered up into the air, waving at Rachel, Kirsty and the king and queen. Then they zipped away in seven different directions, heading into the human world to their special environments.

"Thank you, girls, for coming up with the idea for the Green Fairies," the king said. "But their work is only just beginning!"

"Yes," the queen agreed. "The world has many environmental problems, and fairies alone will never be able to solve them all. We need human help!"

"We'll carry on doing our best," Rachel promised. But Kirsty was frowning. "Will it be enough, though?" she asked sadly. "There's so much to do!

There's the polluted air, the melting ice caps, the damaged coral reefs, the rubbish on the beaches and in the rivers and the parks, and the destruction of the rainforest."

"What can two girls and seven fairies *really* do to save the planet?" Rachel sighed.

The queen put her arms around the girls. "Every person's effort makes a difference!" she told them. "If you each get some of your friends to do their part to help the environment, and then those friends tell some more friends and so on…just imagine what a big impact that will make. And it will all start with two smart young girls like *you*!"

Seeds of Hope

Rachel and Kirsty glanced at each other, both feeling a rush of pride. Then the king beckoned Bertram to come forward. On the wand tray were two little green bags the girls hadn't noticed before. The queen handed one of the bags to Rachel and one to Kirsty.

"Take a look inside," the queen said with a smile.

Curiously, the girls peeked inside the bags. Inside were some small golden seeds.

"They're magic seeds," the king explained. "If you plant them and care for them, they'll grow into big strong trees, a memory of your adventures with the Green Fairies!"

"We'll plant them as soon as we get home," Kirsty promised.

"And they'll remind us that we need to look after the Earth!" added Rachel.

"Thank you again, girls," the queen said, lifting her wand. "Now it's time to send you home!"

As a mist of fairy dust swirled around
the girls, they waved goodbye to their
Fairyland friends. Just a few seconds
later, Rachel and Kirsty found themselves
back in the garden of their cottage. The
sun was now shining brightly, and almost
all the frost had melted.

"Oh, there you are!" said Mr Walker, staggering out of the front door with two heavy suitcases. "We're ready to leave."

Rachel's mum and Kirsty's parents followed him out of the cottage.

"Hasn't it been a wonderful holiday, girls?" Kirsty's dad said with a smile.

Kirsty and Rachel nodded eagerly.

"And now we have lots of ideas about how we can help the environment!" Kirsty replied. "We're going to pick up litter, and recycle more stuff wherever we can."

"We're going to try to save energy by turning off lights," Rachel added. "And can we walk more and take public transport instead of using the car sometimes? We're also going to ask our teachers if we can learn more about the environment and hold fundraising events, and all kinds of other things!"

"That's very impressive, girls!" Mrs Tate smiled. "But why have you suddenly become so interested in the environment?"

Rachel and Kirsty glanced knowingly at each other.

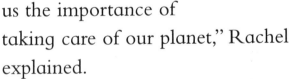

"Oh, we met some people here on Rainspell who've shown us the importance of taking care of our planet," Rachel explained.

"That's great!" said Mrs Walker. "We'll help you all we can."

The girls shared a secret smile. What an amazing week it had been!

"It's a shame we have to say goodbye, Rachel," Kirsty said with a sigh. "But we'll see each other again soon, won't we?"

Rachel nodded. "Of course we will," she exclaimed. "After all, we're going to have lots more wonderful adventures with our magical fairy friends!"

Now it's time for Kirsty and Rachel to help...

Milly the River Fairy

Read on for a sneak peek...

"Ooh, it's definitely colder than yesterday," Rachel Walker said, as she and her best friend Kirsty Tate strolled through Rainspell Park. "I can't believe we were so warm on the beach at the start of the week – and today we're all wrapped up in our woollies!"

Kirsty grinned at Rachel. "And *I* can't believe we were swimming in the sea with Coral the Reef Fairy a few days ago," she said in a low voice. "Imagine how freezing cold the water must be right now!"

Rachel shivered at the thought. "She'd have to use a *lot* of fairy magic to keep us warm today, wouldn't she?"

The two girls smiled at each other as they walked on through the park. It was the autumn half-term, and they were both here on Rainspell Island for a week with their parents. Rainspell Island was the place where Kirsty and Rachel had first met. They'd shared a very magical summer together, and now this holiday was turning out to be every bit as magical! "Oh, I do love being friends with the fairies," Kirsty said happily, thinking about all the exciting adventures they'd had so far. "We really are the luckiest girls in the world, Rachel."

"Definitely," Rachel agreed. Golden-brown leaves were tumbling from the trees in the park every time the wind blew, and she noticed just then that some of the trees were already bare. "Well, it's certainly windy enough today to sail our boats, anyway," she said, as a yellow horse chestnut leaf floated down and landed at her feet. She glanced at the paper boat she was holding. The girls had each made one back at their holiday cottage that morning. "They're going to whizz along with this breeze behind them..."

Read Milly the River Fairy to find out
what adventures are in store for Kirsty and Rachel!

Meet the
Green Fairies

Jack Frost's goblins make a mess everywhere they
go. Can Kirsty and Rachel clean things up
before the natural world is seriously harmed?

www.rainbowmagicbooks.co.uk

Meet the fairies, play games
and get sneak peeks at
the latest books!

www.rainbowmagicbooks.co.uk

There's fairy fun for everyone on
our wonderful website.
You'll find great activities, competitions, stories and
fairy profiles, and also a special newsletter.

Get 30% off all Rainbow Magic books at

www.rainbowmagicbooks.co.uk

Enter the code RAINBOW at the checkout.
Offer ends 31 December 2012.

Offer valid in United Kingdom and Republic of Ireland only.

Win Rainbow Magic Goodies!

There are lots of Rainbow Magic fairies, and we want to know which one is your favourite! Send us a picture of her and tell us in thirty words why she is your favourite and why you like Rainbow Magic books. Each month we will put the entries into a draw and select one winner to receive a Rainbow Magic Sparkly T-shirt and Goody Bag!

Send your entry on a postcard to Rainbow Magic Competition, Orchard Books, 338 Euston Road, London NW1 3BH.
Australian readers should email: childrens.books@hachette.com.au
New Zealand readers should write to Rainbow Magic Competition, 4 Whetu Place, Mairangi Bay, Auckland NZ.
Don't forget to include your name and address.
Only one entry per child.

Good luck!

Meet the
Ocean Fairies

Ally
the Dolphin
Fairy

Amelie
the Seal
Fairy

Pia
the Penguin
Fairy

Tess
the Sea Turtle
Fairy

Stephanie
the Starfish
Fairy

Whitney
the Whale
Fairy

Courtney
the Clownfish
Fairy

Naughty goblins have smashed the magical conch
shell! Kirsty and Rachel must restore it
so that the oceans can have harmony again.

www.rainbowmagicbooks.co.uk